"It's a trap—and I'm the bait?" Havok screamed.

"How brilliant you are, Alex," Cameron Hodge sneered. "When your friends come to save you, they will find you have become a mutate slave. And that will be their fate as well! And for your brother, Scott Summers, I have an especially ingenious plan. Genegineer, proceed with the mutate Havok's mental implants!"

"I must warn you again, Hodge," the Genegineer said nervously. "The implants may not work."

"Shut up!" Hodge spat. "I want this man to lead the battle against the X-Men. So long as the X-Men live, I will never be able to fully control the world's mutant population. Scott Summers will face Alex, his own brother, in battle—something I cannot wait to witness!"

X-Tinction Agenda

adapted by Vicki Kamida

based on stories by Chris Claremont
and Louise Simonson

cover illustration by Dana and Del Thompson

text illustrations by Aristides Ruiz

Bullseye Books

Random House 🏠 New York

X-MEN®

X-Tinction Agenda

CHAPTER ONE

Inside the Danger Room of Professor Xavier's School for Gifted Youngsters, a dramatic fight was taking place between the X-Men Jean Grey and her good friend, Ororo, otherwise known as Storm.

"The thunderstorm you've created is very impressive," Jean said. "But I think a focused telekinetic shot to the solar plexus—"

Jean lined up her aim and directed a blast of her powerful mental energy right at Storm's stomach. The wind and rain that Storm had generated disappeared. Storm herself dropped through the air, saved from a crash landing only by the cape she wore.

"—might prove a bit more effective," Jean

finished. "Care to concede the match to me?"

"Quite the contrary," a smiling Storm said, picking herself up off the floor of the Danger Room. "I have barely begun!"

Summoning all her own mutant super-powers, Ororo called up a winter storm.

"It's freezing!" Jean cried. "I can feel it even through my insulated costume."

All the rain Storm had commanded earlier turned to freezing ice. Now, every surface of the Danger Room was slick and slippery. Jean stumbled backward, and immediately began to slide. Storm blew a gust of wind at her friend.

"A disadvantage of telekinesis is that you need to focus your concentration in order to use it," said Storm. "I no longer intend to allow you that opportunity."

From a control booth high in the wall above the Danger Room, Scott Summers—also known as Cyclops—and Forge watched their teammate slip and slide on the ice. In the Danger Room's holographic simulation, Jean was perched on the roof of a tall building. Storm's burst of cold air pushed Jean to the very brink of the roof.

"Wave goodbye, Jean," Ororo said, saluting her friend. "And happy landings!"

With a final gust of wind, Storm sent Jean flying. In the control booth, Forge watched the fight with a stern expression on his face. Scott Summers, meanwhile, winced as Jean hit bottom with an audible groan.

"We should cancel this sequence," Forge said. He went to press a red button on the console. But Scott stopped him.

"Both Jean and Storm need the practice," Scott said. "The sequence ends when one of them gives up." Through his protective ruby quartz sunglasses, Scott watched the two women fight.

All of the X-Men were mutants, beings with superhuman powers. In these Danger Room simulations, the X-Men tested their strengths and honed their skills. Their leader and teacher, Professor Xavier, urged his students to keep their powers in topnotch condition. If the X-Men were going to fight to defend mutantkind, to promote justice and understanding for all mutants, their skills would have to be razor-sharp.

Storm could control the weather, and Jean could move objects and people with her telekinetic powers and read minds with telepathy. Cyclops was able to focus a laser beam from his eyes and blast anything in sight. When he wasn't in costume, he wore sunglasses that helped contain his powerful optic energy.

Forge turned his gaze back to the battle. Storm was the leader of the X-Men, but she was also his good friend. Forge's specialty was inventing highly sophisticated weapons and computer technology. Right now, he wanted nothing more than to see Storm come out of this test unharmed.

"Jean's as good as she ever was," Scott commented.

The icy wind cleared and both men saw that Storm had Jean in a whirlwind. Storm was spinning her teammate so fast and hard that Jean didn't have a clue which end was up.

"You were saying, pal?" Forge countered.

Two faces appeared on the Danger Room's

video monitor. "Cable and Rahne requesting access to the Danger Room," the white-haired man said. Cable was also a mutant. One of his arms was bionic, and in the other he hoisted a powerful plasma gun.

Rahne Sinclair, the girl beside him, had short red hair, pointy ears, and a fearsome expression on her face. In her thick Scottish accent, Rahne said, "Ye dinna say ye'd be using the Room all afternoon!"

"We're still running the sequence," Forge told them through the intercom. "Sorry, but you'll have to wait."

Cable glared into the video monitor. Rahne, meanwhile, pounded her fist into her hand. "If the Professor were here, I promise ye he'd set the X-Men right. What about *our* training, eh?"

"Well, the Professor isn't here," Cable told her. "That means we're on our own."

Although they often worked with the X-Men, Cable and Rahne were actually members of a different team, the New Mutants. At the moment, the X-Men and the New Mutants seemed to be having trouble sharing the same space. And that was rubbing Cable the wrong way.

Inside the Danger Room, Storm kept Jean Grey spinning on her powerful whirlwind. Suddenly, the wind died down to a small gust and Ororo crumpled, falling toward the floor.

"What's going on?" Cyclops demanded, checking the Room's control board. "I'm getting a reading that Storm's powers have completely shut down."

Forge reached for the power switch. Just as he did, Jean regained her balance and sent a protective telekinetic shield to catch Storm. Instantly, Ororo stopped falling. Jean flew below Storm and caught her.

"Not to worry, guys," Jean said. "I have her."

"...Couldn't stay aloft," Storm was murmuring. "Body felt like it had turned to lead...couldn't form a wind to hold me..."

"What happened?" Scott wanted to know. "Why did Storm lose control?"

Forge reviewed a video playback of the

session, while Jean carried Ororo toward the Danger Room's exit.

"As far as I can tell, Storm used too much power too quickly," said Forge. "In her desire to give Jean the ride of her life, I'm afraid our friend overdid it."

Just as Jean and Storm got to the exit, Cable came bursting through the door. Rahne was by his side. Cable's plasma gun was raised—and loaded.

"It's time for *our* workout!" Cable bellowed. "So could everyone else please vacate the premises—now!"

Behind him, Rahne shook her fist in the air. "That's telling 'em, laddie!"

"This is our home too, Cable," Jean said, making way for him. "We all have to get along."

"Look," said Cable. "Somebody had to take charge of the New Mutants. None of you hotshots wanted the job, so it fell to me. That includes insisting we get our training. Any objections?"

"Your points are well taken," Storm said.

"But if we are to accept your leadership of the New Mutants, then you must also accept that your team is part of a greater whole. Like it or not, these facilities must be shared. For now, however, the Danger Room is yours."

While Rahne and Cable went through their training session, Storm and Jean set up a picnic on the grounds of Professor Xavier's school. Scott was there too, along with his brother, Alex. They spread their blankets by the lake and devoured their lunch.

"Cable will learn to get along with us," Scott insisted. "He just has a different style."

Jean sighed. "If the Professor were here, he'd say the right thing and we'd all be able to get along." She stood up and collected her belongings. "That's enough fun in the sun for me. I'm going back inside."

"I'll come with you," said Scott. "We need to plan tomorrow's sequence. It's you versus me, babe. I hope you're ready!"

"Oh, please!" said Jean, punching Scott in the arm. "You're the one who should look out tomorrow."

As Jean and Scott walked away, Alex tossed a rock into the lake. Alex's mutant ability to channel cosmic rays into energy blasts had earned him the name Havok. But being Cyclops' younger brother didn't leave Alex much room on the team. Alex wanted his own important spot with the X-Men. Storm had often reassured him that his chance would come, but Alex was impatient.

"I hate just sitting around like this!" he said.

"I hear ye!" Rahne said, suddenly coming upon them.

At first, Storm and Alex were startled. Rahne was still in her wolfgirl state from her Danger Room exercise. As the shapeshifting Wolfsbane, Rahne was capable of ferocious destruction with her vicious teeth and claws. Now, Rahne went from wolfgirl to her fully human state.

"Sorry to startle ye," she said. "Jean and Scott said I might find ye out here. I wanted tae thank ye fer letting us use the Danger

Room for our practice, Storm."

"I hope we all find a way to work together," said Storm. "No member of the team is any less important than any other—"

Storm was about to go on when an explosive roar came from the trees behind them. There was a flash of light, and the thunderous sound of very loud engines approaching.

"What on earth!" Storm shouted.

Another blast shot through the trees. The force knocked all three off their feet.

"They're down!" came a cry.

"Let's keep 'em that way!" came another.

Three heavily armed high-tech military vehicles roared into the clearing. Their drivers wore helmets and carried high-powered weapons.

"Who *are* those fellas?" Rahne cried.

"Terrorists! They've got ultra-performance assault vehicles!" said Alex as he stumbled to his feet.

One of the drivers fired off another nasty blast from his weapon. Alex went down again.

"We can't face them in the open," Storm

warned. "Get under cover. Head for the woods! They can't follow us there." She fled and the other two followed.

"Wanna bet, lassie?" Rahne cried, looking back over her shoulder.

The military vehicles were crashing through the trees in hot pursuit. "This is your only warning!" the lead driver called out. "Surrender immediately or be shot down!"

To prove his point, the driver sent another bolt of energy their way.

Alex stopped dead in his tracks. "We can fight them," he insisted. Summoning his power, Alex directed a blast of cosmic energy at the lead vehicle. First came the flash, and then the blinding heat. The force sent the driver flying.

"Nice one!" Rahne said. She had already started her transformation into pure wolf. Hunched over in an animal stance, with her fangs and claws bared, Rahne growled, "Let me at 'em!"

The two remaining drivers came at them full force. Storm knew the rest of the X-Men

would be responding to the noise any moment now. If they could fight off these intruders, even for a short time, help would arrive.

Wolfsbane was already on one of the drivers. She tore at him ferociously. Havok was striking the one he'd dismounted with another plasma blast.

Storm got ready to direct a gale-force hurricane at the third intruder. Suddenly, the driver sent a net spinning out at her.

"Look out!" Havok called.

Storm tried to fight off the web, but it was no use. A moment later, she was completely tangled up in it. The ropes tightened around her arms and legs, leaving her unable to use any of her powers effectively.

"First catch-web enabled," Storm's attacker announced. He unleashed two more, trapping both Rahne and Havok.

"Initiate upload immediately!" the lead intruder ordered.

"All targets digitized," Storm's attacker confirmed.

The third terrorist spoke into the communications headset she wore. "Prisoners secured. Location secure. Limited time before mutie reinforcements gather. Recommend proceeding with transport."

"Get ready, genejokes," the first intruder told his prisoners. "You shoulda run while you had the chance."

"Ye had better explain yerselves," Rahne growled.

"I think I understand," said Storm. She recognized their captors' uniforms. She'd seen files about these intruders in Professor X's Ready Room. "These are Genoshan Magistrates. And we are their prisoners."

"For a mutie, you sure are smart," sneered the female magistrate. "Now shut up. You've got a trip to take!"

The head magistrate sent a series of commands through his control panel. There was a flash and a pulse of energy. And then Storm, Rahne, and Havok—along with their Genoshan captors—were gone.

CHAPTER TWO

The country of Genosha was an island nation, east of Africa. Once it had been barren rock, lacking even the most elementary natural resources. Over time, it became a prosperous jewel in the Indian Ocean—thanks to the efforts of a slave population.

These slaves had originally been mutants—superpowered human beings. But the leaders of Genosha imprisoned these mutants. Then the mutants were specially bioengineered, and their minds were wiped clean of all their memories. The mutates' latent powers were developed and enhanced, and their wills were enslaved, forcibly turned to the enrichment of the state.

It was at the Citadel, headquarters of Genoshan State Security, that the mutates were engineered and controlled. Within the Citadel, it was the job of the Genegineer to transform Genoshans with mutant abilities into slave mutates.

But it was Cameron Hodge, leader of Genosha, who ruled the Citadel. He decided who would be the next victims of the Genegineer's terrible transformations. Hodge controlled who would live, who would die— and who would become a mutate, forced to serve the state.

Now, in a room deep within the Citadel, Hodge and his Genegineer greeted their X-Men visitors. "You mutants are prisoners of Genosha," the Genegineer said.

"We demand to be released," Storm cried. "Under what pretense do you hold us?"

Cameron Hodge spoke from the dark corner where he stood. "What a stupid question!" he cried out. "You have been brought here so that you will never again be able to wreak your mutant havoc upon an unsuspecting and defenseless world."

"Who are you?" Rahne cried out. "What kind of man do ye call yerself?"

For the first time, Hodge revealed himself to his prisoners. All three gasped.

Once, Hodge had been an ordinary human, with an ordinary body. But the X-Man Archangel had cut off Hodge's head with his razor-sharp wings. Cybernetics experts had constructed a mechanical body for Hodge— very strong, and very deadly.

The man's head was attached with thick cables to a mechanized, crablike body. When Hodge moved, his six appendages clattered and whirred like machines. Powerful tentacles whipped around him. In front, two sharp tusks hung almost to the floor and glinted even in the dim light.

Rahne tried to throw Hodge off balance, preparing to attack. Instead, she swiftly found herself held aloft in Hodge's viselike grip.

"You don't have the ability to prevail against me!" Hodge told her sharply. His scarred, hideous face twisted in anger. Behind thick glasses, Hodge's mad eyes gleamed. "Wipeout! Take out their powers!" he ordered.

Another man appeared from out of the darkness. He was short and squat and carried a huge weapon. It looked like an oversized machine gun. But in reality the weapon was capable of blocking the use of all mutant superpowers.

"Prepare to lose all your strength!" Wipeout declared.

"That I cannot allow!" Storm cried, and willed herself to create a thunderstorm.

If she could send a bolt of lightning at Hodge's mechanized body, perhaps it would disarm the man. But before she could muster up her powers, Wipeout was already at work. In an instant, the man had zapped all three of them with blasts of energy from his gun. Storm, Rahne, and Havok fell to the ground.

"Why are you doing this?" Storm demanded. "What have we done to you?"

"I have never forgotten what your friend Archangel did to me. I have long sought my vengeance," Hodge explained. "More than that, I know that so long as the X-Men live, I will never be able to fully control the world's mutant population. When your friends come to save you, they will find you have become mutate slaves. And that will be their fate as well."

"It's a trap—and we're the bait!" Havok exclaimed.

"How brilliant," Hodge sneered. "That's exactly what this is. And for your brother, Scott Summers, I have an especially ingenious plan. Genegineer, proceed with the mutate Havok's mental implants!"

"I must warn you again, Hodge," the Genegineer said nervously. "The implants may not work. There is no guarantee that we will be able to erase all the mutant's memories."

"Shut up!" Hodge spat. "I want this man to serve the state as a magistrate, and I want him to lead the battle against the X-Men. Scott Summers will face Alex, his own brother, in battle—something I cannot wait to witness!"

Storm and Rahne stood looking on as Alex was strapped into the Genegineer's awful memory-clearing machine. Havok resisted with all his might, but without his powers he was helpless. Alex was unable to summon even a weak plasma blast.

A giant clamp descended and grabbed Havok's waist. The Genegineer stepped toward the control panel at his feet.

"I beg you," the scientist pleaded. "Your plan may backfire."

"Wipe his memory clean!" Hodge ordered, skittering across the floor on his six-legged mechanized body. "Replace everything with the memories of a Genoshan magistrate. Implant a terrible hatred for his brother, Cyclops. Do it! Now!"

The machine began to hum. Lights on the control panel flashed. Then crackling bolts of electricity began to dance over Havok's body.

In less than five minutes, the Genegineer switched off the machine. Magistrates entered the room and set Alex free. With their weapons they directed him away from the machine.

Havok grabbed a gun from one of them

and aimed it at them. "Is that any way to treat a superior magistrate?" he demanded.

"Excellent!" Hodge shouted. "Such total control! Such victory! And yet, we must not let ourselves get carried away."

Hodge crawled across the room and stood before a giant video monitor. On the screen, Storm saw her fellow X-Men arriving on a remote Genoshan shoreline.

"They are coming," Hodge announced. "Just as I predicted. Magistrate Summers, take up your command."

"You monster!" Rahne cried out, lunging at the man.

"Monster, am I?" Hodge replied. With his mechanical claw, Hodge hurled Rahne against the far wall. She slumped to the floor, unconscious. Hodge's mad eyes blazed. "I'll deal with you later. For now, I want to be sure that these invaders are destroyed. You have your orders, Magistrate Summers."

"Yes, sir," Alex said, saluting Hodge. "I will destroy them." He left the room, followed by two magistrates. The third remained. Hodge gave him the orders to remove Storm and Rahne to a jail cell.

"Their transmodation will have to wait," Hodge said, settling in before the video screen. "Right now, I want to focus my concentration on the lovely battle that is about to take place. I will save my revenge on Storm and Wolfsbane for later."

As Storm was led from Hodge's central command room, she thought, *We are at the mercy of a madman! We must escape!*

On the shores of Genosha, the X-Men were unloading their aircraft, the Blackbird. Cyclops was there, along with Forge, Cable, Wolverine, Archangel, and Jean Grey.

When they had heard the fight back at the mansion, the six mutants had gone looking for their friends. They found only an empty clearing and the remains of the transporter burst that had carried the group to Genosha. A few minutes later, a message from Hodge had come through to the mansion's command room. Hodge claimed responsibility for taking

Storm, Rahne, and Alex captive. Not long after that, the X-Men had mobilized.

Archangel, normally cool and collected, was impatient, anxious to do battle with his nemesis, Cameron Hodge.

"My wings may not have destroyed him in the past," Archangel told his friends, "but this time I plan to slice that demon to bits!"

With that, Archangel flew above the group. Soon he was so high that his blue-and-purple costume and his steel-feathered wings were barely visible.

"That guy's got a grudge a mile long," Wolverine growled. "Let's hope he keeps us in sight. Ever since Hodge told us that Storm, Rahne, and Alex were here, I've smelled a trap." Holding up his fist, Wolverine bared his claws and beamed at them proudly. "Time to sharpen up the old adamantium!"

Wolverine was short and stocky. Beneath his yellow-and-blue mask, patches of thick hair covered his cheeks, giving his face a distinctly wolfish quality. Wolverine's skeleton was laced with adamantium, the strongest metal that existed. With his mutant healing factor and his foot-long razor-sharp claws, Wolverine was one of the most powerful—and most fierce—of all the X-Men.

"How far to the Citadel?" Jean asked.

"About forty miles," Cyclops replied.

"Of course, Forge decided it was necessary to pack everything—including the kitchen sink," complained Cable. He lugged a box from the X-Men's plane and dropped it onto the beach.

"Don't look at *me*," Forge protested. "It was Cyclops' idea. I just tinkered together a few gadgets he thought we might need."

"Which we will deploy as soon as we near the Citadel," Cyclops added. He went to stand on a rise and looked inland. Cliffs towered above the beach. There was a pass between them that opened onto a clearing.

"Jean, you hook up with Archangel and fly lookout," Cyclops said. "The rest of us should be careful. We're entering a natural amphitheater. I agree with Wolverine—we need to be on guard against an ambush. If ever there was a place for one, this is it!"

Jean Grey flew off to catch up with Archangel. Forge, Cable, and Wolverine shouldered the X-Men's supplies. Cyclops took a box and led the group between the cliffs.

From a point above the group, Magistrate Alex Summers observed the arriving X-Men. In his new identity as magistrate, Alex Summers was in charge of firing on his former teammates, including his brother Scott. Quickly, Alex planned the Genoshan attack.

"Let's do this by the book," Alex told his squadron. "The one in front is their leader, Cyclops. Disable him first. Then we'll move in and take out the group. Ready, aim, fire!"

The squadron unleashed a powerful series of blasts from their weapons. Down below, the X-Men scattered for cover behind the rocks.

"Take them out!" Alex ordered.

He led the squadron down off the cliffs and into the clearing. By now, the X-Men were unloading their own weapons and ammunition. Archangel and Jean had already flown back to the group.

Cable was ready first. He pumped countless plasma bursts into the arriving magistrates.

From a distance, Jean Grey used a telekinetic blast to send a shower of rocks down upon the Genoshan commander. But to her surprise, he fought back with an energy burst of his own.

Cyclops came to Jean's rescue. Across the battlefield, the Genoshan unleashed another burst at Cyclops, but it left him unharmed.

"Two can play at this game!" Cyclops cried. He focused his optic blast on the enemy, but the man didn't fall.

"You're powerful, mutant, I'll give you that," the commander cried out. "But your optic blast seems as ineffective on me as my plasma blast is on you!"

"Alex!" Cyclops cried.

Now that they were closer, Scott Summers recognized his younger brother instantly. All around them, the magistrates did battle with the other X-Men. The two brothers faced each other—as mortal enemies.

Scott Summers struggled with his younger

brother, gripping Alex's face between his hands. "Listen to me, Alex!" Cyclops cried. "I'm Scott, your brother!"

"My brother—a mutant terrorist?" Alex sneered. "Don't make me laugh!"

"What's happened to you?" Scott cried. "Why can't you remember?"

Alex shot out with his fist, cutting a blow to Scott Summers's jaw. Cyclops reeled from the shock. "I know who I am," Alex said. "I'm a magistrate! A Genoshan! You're Genosha's enemy, and that makes you my enemy too!"

"You always were too stubborn for your own good," Scott growled. His fists raised, he fought back with his own blows. "Listen to me, Alex! Try to *think*. Your plasma bursts don't harm me, and my optic blasts don't hurt you! We just make each other stronger. Why do you think that is?"

By now, Scott had wrestled Alex to the ground. He pinned him with his knees. His hands closed around his brother's neck.

"Answer me, bright boy," Scott demanded. "Why? I'll tell you. It's because you're my

brother, and we're genetically immune to each other's powers!"

Alex grimaced. "Lies! Mutant lies!"

"There's only one way I can pound some sense into that thick head of yours," Scott said through gritted teeth. He banged Alex's head against the ground. "It worked when we were little, and it'll work now. Even if I have to crack your thick skull, I'm going to force the truth into it!"

Through all his rage and pain, Alex Summers had an uneasy feeling. *Can what he says be true?*

An instant later, though, a murderous fury rose up in him. Fighting with all his might, he managed to free himself from Cyclops' grip.

"It's impossible!" Alex shouted. "I was born here. You can't trick me like this! Magistrates—time to transport. Now!"

There was a burst of light as a Genoshan transporter blasted the entire magistrate squad out of the battlcfield. A moment later, the X-Men stood speechless inside the empty clearing.

"What just happened?" Archangel asked.

"They teleported," Jean informed him. "That was probably how they got here."

Scott Summers was still shaken from the encounter with his brother. He pounded his fists into the ground where they had been fighting not a moment earlier. "It's all wrong," Cyclops said. "Alex—my own brother—is a magistrate, fighting alongside the Genoshans. He doesn't have a clue who he really is!"

"That means someone has it in for us personally," Wolverine observed.

"And that someone is Cameron Hodge," Archangel added, his blue face set in anger.

"They knew our location," Forge remarked. "That means satellite surveillance. I'll put together scramblers to protect us."

"I know we'd planned to circle around secretly, but..." Cable began.

"You're right," Scott said. For the moment, he made himself set aside his feelings about his brother, and became the leader once again. "They know we're coming. There's nothing stopping us from moving in on 'em now—fast and ugly. Let's do it!" They moved swiftly toward their target—the Citadel.

From his vantage point in the Citadel, Cameron Hodge observed the X-Men on his video screen. They collected their weapons and ammunition and prepared to march toward Hammer Bay, Genosha's capital.

"Mutant fools!" he exclaimed. "How can you plan when you don't even know what your enemies are capable of? I will destroy you, as one of you has destroyed me. With Genosha as my base, I will obliterate your mutant race from the earth."

An evil grin spread across Hodge's hideous face, as he watched the X-Men's progress.

"Good luck, Cyclops," he said. "You think that in fighting your brother, you have faced the worst. Fool! I planned Havok's defeat at your own hands. I have also insured that he will be shamed by that loss. Now he has something to prove. His demonstration of loyalty to Genosha will betray you all—right into my hands!"

CHAPTER THREE

While Hodge contemplated his devious plan, the Genegineer was busy putting Storm and Rahne onto transmodation platforms. Once the two were securely strapped down, the Genegineer approached his commander.

"Subjects Wolfsbane and Storm are ready for transmodation," he informed Hodge.

"Excellent!" Hodge cackled.

Genosha's leader moved across the floor to where Storm and Rahne were clamped down. Both women were wearing skintight mutate slave suits. Storm's was yellow and white, and had the number 20 written on it. Rahne's was orange and black and had the number 490 on its chest.

"As I have told you, once the process is complete," the Genegineer explained, "these suits will be bonded to them like a second skin—"

"—and Storm and Wolfsbane will no longer exist," Hodge finished for him. "Instead, Genosha will add two mutate slaves to its population."

For both Storm and Rahne, Hodge's plan was a nightmare that would not end. Already, mutates had shaved their heads, and restructured certain genetic material within their brains. The Genegineer would use this material in the transmodation process to create biological syntheses—combining their own genetics with mutate properties. The result: the two of them would be turned into utterly controllable mutate slaves!

"Get on with it, Genegineer!" Hodge ordered. Sneering, he leaned in close to the two women. "Probe their minds! Mutate them! Wipe them clear of memories, of everything!"

"As you wish, Commander," the Genegineer replied. He stepped toward the control

panel to begin the transmodation.

"No, wait." Hodge stopped him. His gaze narrowed and he stared into Rahne's almond-shaped eyes. "I want this one to know, in some dark corner of her mind, who she was and that she is now helpless to oppose my will."

"That's much too dangerous, Hodge," the Genegineer protested. "She'll be a walking powder keg. Your insane desire for revenge will blow up in all of our faces. You're putting the entire Genoshan society at risk!"

"I didn't ask for your opinion, Genegineer," Hodge shot back. "What I ask for is results!"

"You willna get away with it," Rahne spat. "The X-Men will rescue us."

"Will they now?" Hodge replied snidely. "Then they had best do it soon, had they not? Initiate mind probe! Now!"

As the genetic transmodation began, Rahne screamed out in agony. Storm would be next.

"That's it, dear Wolfsbane," Hodge crowed. "Scream! Fight it! I want you to remember, in some part of the wasteland that will be your mind, that it was I—Cameron Hodge—who caused you such horror and such pain!"

Moments later, the waves of energy slowed to a halt. The Genegineer released the clamp that held Rahne down. Slowly, she sat up, then got to her feet. All the life had gone from her eyes. All the resistance had left her body. Instead, Rahne was like a robot, a zombie.

"Take a long look," Hodge spat at Storm. "This will be your fate, too, and that of all the X-Men!"

"Commander Hodge, I must protest," the Genegineer broke in. "Your obsession with the X-Men will destroy us!"

"It is your *weakness* that will ruin us!" Hodge countered. "Begin Storm's transmodation. Or else I will!"

Reluctantly, the Genegineer approached Storm's transmodation platform. When he stood near enough, Storm made her plea— softly, so that Hodge would not hear.

"I know you think you owe Hodge your loyalty, but the man is a lunatic," she whispered. "He'll stop at nothing."

Storm saw a look of relief and understanding pass over the Genegineer's face, and felt encouraged. "It is up to you to prevent this insanity from taking place. I beg you: *do* something, anything. Whatever it takes to stop him."

"I cannot help you," the Genegineer replied softly. "What you're asking is impossible. It's too late."

"What's this?" Hodge demanded. "Why have you stopped? I told you to begin the process. Now!"

As Hodge looked on with an evil grin, the Genegineer started the transmodation. Storm's words were in his ears. There might be a way to stop Hodge and his devious plan.

At the last minute, before the transmodation was finished, the Genegineer made a slight adjustment to the process. The change was so small that Hodge would never notice— at least, not until the moment came. He hoped by then it would not be too late—for Storm, for himself, and for Genosha.

✧　　✧　　✧　　✧　　✧　　✧　　✧

In a warehouse across town, the X-Men were busy planning their strategy for breaking into the Citadel to free their comrades. Cyclops had just finished explaining his idea to the others.

"It's a good scheme, Summers," said Cable. "Those with quiet powers set the charges and locate the prisoners. Those of you with sound-and-light powers can come in afterward and act as shock troops."

Cable loaded his weapon and prepared his ammunition. Forge put the finishing touches on a series of robot auto-bombs. "Once I release these," he explained to Cyclops, "they'll seek out the Citadel's technological center—and wipe it out!"

"Nice work, bub," said Wolverine. He watched his fellow X-Men pack up the bombs. "But I gotta tell you, Cyke, you should let me go with the first wave!"

"That's not the plan," said Cyclops. "That phase of the mission is search. I want you to stick around here and be part of the *destroy*."

"Yeah, yeah," said Wolverine, watching Jean pack. "I heard the plan."

Cable, Jean, and Forge prepared to leave the warehouse. As they headed out, Cyclops, Wolverine, and Archangel wished them well. The three remaining X-Men planned to monitor the progress of their friends. Once they were safely inside the Citadel, Cyclops, Wolverine, and Archangel would follow.

For Jean, Cable, and Forge, the trip across Hammer Bay was short—and tense. All three kept their eyes and ears open for any sign of Genoshan magistrates. But they arrived at the Citadel without incident.

Jean Grey hovered above the building. Using her telekinetic powers, she moved Forge and Cable into position inside the Citadel's courtyard. Cable stood guard, with his very powerful—and very quiet—plasma gun, while Forge gained an entry into the building. Silently, he released his robot auto-bombs through the opening. The machines would seek out their destinations. Later, they would detonate at preset times.

From her watch high above the Citadel, Jean spotted a magistrate. The guard was looking right at Forge and Cable! Jean sent them a telepathic warning. "Look out!" she cried. "There's a guard on the balcony!"

Immediately, Forge and Cable took cover. To protect them from being seen, Jean shot a telepathic burst at the guard. The magistrate let out an earth-shattering cry, alerting his fellow Genoshans.

Without warning, a swarm of magistrates came running from all directions. The X-Men were heavily outnumbered. Cable attacked with all his bionically enhanced power. Jean flew among the magistrates, taking them out one by one with telepathic bursts. Forge had reserved ammunition packs, which he now turned on the magistrates.

"No way are you guys gonna win this one," Cable asserted. He shot round after round of plasma at the magistrate squadron. As individual soldiers came at him, Cable fought them off with powerful blows.

"We are vastly outnumbered here," Forge

advised. "Even the advanced weaponry I brought along may not help us!"

The courtyard filled with the roar of battle. Weapons and bodies fell everywhere. Jean was searching desperately for a plan when a huge, evil-looking machine entered the courtyard. In the very center of the six-legged monstrosity sat a human head!

"Cameron Hodge!" Jean gasped.

"That's right," Hodge cried out. "What a pity this battle must end so abruptly. Wipeout, block their powers!"

The squat man stood before Cable and Forge. A field of energy came from his specially designed weapon. A second later, Cable and Forge slumped to the ground, unconscious.

With Forge and Cable out of commission, Wipeout turned his attention to Jean Grey. She felt the flash of Wipeout's power, and then she, too, dropped.

For the first time in years, Jean found herself without her telepathic abilities. She tried to tap into Hodge's mind. But her mental powers came up empty.

Jean looked at her colleagues in horror. Without their powers, they were helpless. Now she knew the fate her teammates had met. Or at least she thought she did.

At that moment, a familiar figure came walking into the courtyard. The young woman was wearing a strange orange-and-black costume, and her eyes were lifeless.

"Mutate, step closer," Hodge urged, his voice taking on a dreadful tone. "I want your would-be saviors to see you!"

"Rahne!" Cable, who had regained his senses, cried. "What have you done to her?"

Hodge cackled. "You'll find out soon enough. Tell them, Mutate 490!"

In a dull voice, the mutated Rahne Sinclair addressed Cable and the X-Men. "Ye are condemned to genetic transmodation. Ye will be transformed into mutate slaves. And ye will serve Genosha loyally—as I myself now serve."

CHAPTER FOUR

"Rahne!" Jean cried out. "Hodge—you've turned her into a monster, a robot—"

"—A loyal slave," Hodge finished for her. "And that will be your fate as well. As soon as I gather all you mutant terrorists—"

Jean drew in a sharp breath, and Hodge went on. "Oh yes, I know about the rest of your little group. Right now, my magistrates are conducting a full-scale attack on your warehouse hideaway. Did you X-Men think you'd be able to escape my surveillance?"

"Just because you have us, Hodge, don't begin to think you'll keep us," Cable asserted. "Or that you've won this war."

"Won?" Hodge asked. "Of course I've won.

Without your powers, the key to victory is no longer yours. I only regret that Forge remains unconscious. Wipeout, answer me! What have you done to him?"

Hodge's assistant quivered. "N-nothing, Commander! I'm blameless, I swear. I did no more to Forge than to these others."

"If I learn that is not the case, I shall make you pay, wormfood," Hodge thundered. "Now out of my sight, you quivering turnip!"

Wipeout ran quickly out of the courtyard. Magistrate reinforcements arrived. Hodge ordered them to put the X-Men in handcuffs.

"Even without your powers," Hodge said, "I don't trust you. You X-Men are just foolish enough to try escaping."

Hodge picked up Forge with one of his tentacles and tossed him at a magistrate. "Since you have nothing better to do with yourself, Magistrate Summers," Hodge said, "you can carry this unconscious mutant trash to his cell!"

"Havok!" Jean cried out. "She hadn't recognized Alex at first in his magistrate uniform. He looked as if in a daze.

"Summers!" said Cable. "Listen to us! Don't you remember who you are?"

But Alex Summers's face remained expressionless. With Forge over his shoulder, he led the group from the courtyard. Cable knew that once they were in their jail cells, the X-Men would have very little chance of escaping. Even though he was handcuffed, he had to do something!

I may not have use of my bionic powers, Cable thought, *but I still have my ordinary strength!*

Hodge had followed the group inside the Citadel. Now, Cable turned around to face their enemy. He looked at the man's hideous face and grotesque body. Summoning all his fury, he snapped apart his handcuffs.

"I only need one hand to rip off your stinking head!" he cried.

With that, Cable lunged for Hodge. He reached for the wires that attached Hodge's head to his mechanized body.

But as soon as he did, Hodge lashed out with an army of tentacles. Suddenly, Cable was trapped in Hodge's grip. A wicked tentacle snapped itself around his face. Cable froze, immobilized by Hodge's cybernetic tricks.

He's got me, Cable thought, grimacing. *Blasted monster has more gadgets than a Swiss army knife!*

"Brilliant attempt, Cable," Hodge said, "but as you see, your efforts are useless."

Hodge flung Cable against the wall of the prison. Then he sent out a hail of spikes from his mechanized body, pinning Cable against the wall.

Hodge's evil smile glinted in the prison's dark hallway. "Perhaps now you X-Men will believe what the mutates Rahne and Storm have already learned—there is no escape!"

"You mutated Storm too?" Jean demanded as Alex Summers tossed her and Forge into their cell.

"You didn't expect me to let her remain her tempestuous self, did you?" Hodge asked sarcastically. "Lock them in!" he ordered. Then he turned to Cable and his malicious grin reappeared. "This one I'll leave pinned to the wall," he said. "As a pleasant reminder to the others of just how extensive my powers are. And when it's time for the next round of transmodations to begin, I promise, Cable, you will be the first!"

By this time, the remaining X-Men were already in place, prepared to make a second strike on the Citadel. From their communications link-up with the others, Cyclops knew that Jean, Forge, and Cable had been captured. He'd heard the entire battle between the X-Men and the Genoshan magistrates on the hidden two-way radio Forge carried. Cyclops had also learned about Rahne's transmodation and Hodge's plan for Jean, Forge, and Cable.

Just outside the Citadel, Cyclops quickly outlined their plan. "Wolverine, you locate the others. Your mission is to release them. Archangel, you head to Hodge's central command. Do your best to shut it down."

"I'll do more than that, if you don't mind," Archangel assured him. "I've been wanting another shot at Hodge ever since I found out he survived our battle. I intend to destroy the man, once and for all."

"Be careful," said Cyclops. "If Hodge turns Wipeout on you, your powers will be useless."

"What's your job?" Wolverine asked.

"I'm going to find my brother and pound some sense into him," Scott Summers vowed. "We need all the help we can get against Hodge, and that includes Havok."

"Good luck," said Wolverine. "Hodge has done a pretty good job brainwashing the kid."

The three X-Men moved into position. So long as Hodge didn't detect them—and Wipeout didn't come along to remove their powers—they stood a chance at success.

Wolverine was the first one inside. He bared his claws: *Snikt!* He wanted to be prepared for whatever greeted him. The foot-long adamantium claws might well cause a magistrate to have second thoughts about attacking *this* member of the X-Men!

While Cyclops and Archangel headed upstairs, Wolverine made his way into the Citadel's gloomy basement. He covered one dark hallway after another, searching for the prison. Even though he was on guard against attack, Wolverine wasn't prepared for the blast that greeted him as he turned a corner.

Four magistrates were standing guard at the end of the hallway. Beyond them, Wolverine saw a row of jail cells. Inside one of them were his teammates!

"Four to one odds. Now that ain't playin' fair!" Wolverine grumbled.

"Full automatic. Shoot to kill!" the magistrate leader ordered.

Wolverine recognized him. "Summers!" he snarled. "You gave the right order, bub. But I'm better than a bunch of stinkin' magistrates—especially when I'm mad!"

Wolverine lunged at the magistrates. One by one, he took them on with a berserker fury. His claws ripped through them. He tore at their flesh until Summers called off the squad of magistrates.

"Stand back," Alex cried. "Give me a clear shot!"

"Be patient, bub," Wolverine growled.

"Your turn's coming! I use these claws, you'll need a whole new head."

Suddenly, Wolverine was wrenched backward. A vicious metal tentacle snapped around his neck and yanked him to the ground.

"Don't waste your time!" Cameron Hodge informed the magistrates. "A little transmodation is what this fellow needs."

Even trapped in Hodge's tentacle, Wolverine managed to take a long, clean swipe at Hodge's face. "Talk is cheap, metal mouth!" he sneered. "We X-Men don't get nailed anywhere near so easily!"

"Nasty, nasteee—" Hodge recoiled from Wolverine's blow. Then he wrapped Wolverine in a dozen more tentacles. Now his prisoner was completely immobilized. "You have made an admirable effort, which was totally wasted," Hodge declared. "Meanwhile, witness first-hand the fate that awaits you."

Leading Wolverine away from the prison cells, Hodge and Summers made their way upstairs. Soon, they were inside the Genegineer's laboratory. There, Wolverine saw his leader, his teammate, his friend.

"See what has happened to your beloved leader, Storm," Hodge taunted. "As you can tell, Storm is no more. What remains is Mutate 20."

The zombie-like Storm approached. Even the battle-hardened Wolverine was shocked at the results of Hodge's evil doings. "Now what shall I do with *you?*" Hodge asked.

The door to Hodge's command room burst open. Scott Summers and Archangel were standing there.

"Nice of you to drop in," Hodge called out across the room. "This saves me some time, doesn't it?"

"And us too," Archangel proclaimed. "I assumed when I sliced off your head, Hodge, that you would die—"

"Yes," Hodge agreed. "But I made a deal with the devil, and his technology proved you wrong."

"—so now I'll just have to finish off the job!" Archangel continued, launching himself at Hodge. He lashed out with his razor-sharp wings in a swift and furious strike.

Scrackt!

For just an instant, Hodge's body phased into intangibility. In the space where Hodge had been standing, Archangel's blow met dead air. A moment later, the machine-man resolidified—with Archangel's metallic wings wrapped within his tentacles.

"You see, Archangel?" Hodge asked. "I am better, am I not?"

Hodge held Archangel's wings in a viselike grip. The mutant struggled to get free, but it was impossible.

"This is just the beginning, archenemy!" Hodge said. "You will scream and plead, but it will not matter."

Archangel twisted and turned. "He's right! I can't break free!"

Now, both Archangel and Wolverine were caught in Hodge's web. It was up to Cyclops to save his teammates. There was only one solution: make his brother Alex see reason, and bring him back to the X-Men's side!

"Alex, listen!" Scott Summers pleaded.

"Remember who you are!"

"I'm not your brother, and I have my orders," Havok insisted.

"Alex—" said Scott.

"Don't call me that!" Alex bellowed. He sent a giant plasma blast at Cyclops. Scott Summers knew there was no point in zapping him back. Havok was as immune to his optic blast as Cyclops was to his brother's plasma effect.

But the gun Havok carried was a different matter! He aimed it at Cyclops.

In a lightning move, Cyclops slammed the gun aside. He twisted Alex's arm, trapping him in his own powerful grasp. "They've stolen your memories and implanted new ones," Scott insisted.

"They can't!" Alex shot back defiantly. "They couldn't!"

"Isn't that the technique they use on mutates, Alex?" Scott demanded. "What's to prevent them from using it on you?"

"Don't be an idiot!" Alex said, trying to squirm free. "Why would they bother?"

Scott held him tight and whispered, "To use you as a weapon against us—against *me!*"

"Weapon—hah! Your forces defeated my vastly superior ones," Alex pointed out. "The Commander himself accused me of weakness. Now you want to make me betray my own country!"

"You don't have anything to prove to that monster Hodge. I'm trying to stop you from betraying yourself," countered Scott. "Alex, remember how, back when we were little, our parents' plane exploded in flames? Our mother pushed us from it with a single parachute between us. I held you just like this. I didn't let you go then, and I won't let you go now."

Somewhere, in the deepest recesses of Alex Summers's memory, these words rang true. He remembered two little boys falling from the sky. Somehow, he knew who they were.

It was true. Cyclops was right. Someone had been messing with his mind, his life. And he knew exactly who it was.

Hodge had been too busy tormenting Archangel and Wolverine to notice the struggle between the two brothers. Now, he realized that Alex was fighting with Scott.

"Magistrate Summers, disarm the fool who calls himself your brother!" Hodge ordered.

There was no way Alex could save Scott without also revealing that his memory had returned. Taking his brother off guard, Alex rammed his elbow into Scott's stomach. Cyclops doubled over. This was the chance Alex needed. Turning quickly, he reached for the gun Cyclops had knocked from his hand. Before Scott could react, Alex had the gun aimed at him. A second later, Hodge had a tentacle wrapped around Scott Summers's neck.

"Excellent work, Magistrate Summers," Hodge said. "I see you hate this mutant who dared to call you brother. Therefore, when he dies, I guarantee it will be by your own hand!"

CHAPTER FIVE

Hodge had all his captives collected and brought into the prison's torture room. Cyclops and Wolverine hung by their wrists, bolted into handcuffs attached to the wall. Archangel and Forge, who was still unconscious, were swinging from the rafters. Hodge's magistrates were just leading Jean Grey and Cable into the room.

"So many toys," Hodge said. He circled the room. His mechanized body practically hummed with delight. "So devilishly hard to decide how best to play with them! Hurry the prisoners along, magistrates. The sooner they're secured, the sooner we can begin the evening's entertainment!"

"Sorry, Hodge!" Cable shouted. "I'm not in a mood for performing!"

Even with his cuffed hands, Cable managed to yank the gun from his magistrate guard. Jean, who picked up her cue in an instant, did the same.

"Without our powers," Cable said, "we'll just have to use their weapons!" He aimed the gun at Hodge.

"Tsk, tsk, tsk," Hodge said. "Correct me if I'm wrong, but haven't I already proven my superiority?"

Cable fired several rounds at Hodge. Jean held off the magistrate guards. But the bullets just bounced off Hodge's metallic shell.

"You need another lesson, eh?" he asked. The monstrosity shot out a dozen tentacles, wrapping Cable in a deadly snare. Cable, still firing, tried to free himself. Hodge reached out with his mechanized claw, plucked up Jean Grey, and held her before him.

"Shoot!" Hodge urged him. "Go ahead. I'll make it easy for you. I won't move. Not an inch. Of course, lovely Jean can't make that promise. That's a nasty gun, Cable. Bet it'll send a bullet right through her and into me."

Hodge released Cable from his tentacles, making it easy for him to act. But Cable knew his chance had passed. There was no way he could shoot Hodge without also harming Jean. He dropped the gun from his hand.

"Drat!" Hodge cried. "Drat and bother! I so wanted to see the look on your face, Cable, when she died and I didn't."

"Leave her alone, Hodge," came Wolverine's hoarse cry. "Why don't you pick on someone your own size!"

"Like you?" Hodge called out, turning his attention to Logan.

"You got it, bub," Wolverine taunted. "Set me free, and then we'll see who's big enough to take you on!"

"I think not," Hodge said. "And just to prove my point—"

He sent a volley of spikes in Wolverine's direction. Logan grimaced as Hodge's weapons surrounded him on the wall. One of the spikes stabbed Wolverine in the leg. As Wolverine bled, Hodge let loose with a cackling laugh.

"Please," Jean Grey begged. "No more! I can't bear this. I will submit myself to transmodation! Will that convince you, Hodge, to spare my friends?"

"Convince me?" Hodge mused. "It's an awfully convenient change of heart, my sweet. I think further interrogation is in order, to make sure this is no trick."

"Interrogation is not necessary," Alex Summers insisted. He took Jean from her magistrate guard. "If the mutant terrorist is freely choosing transmodation, we must put her in the Genegineer's hands."

Hodge's eyes narrowed, but at last he relented. "Far be it from me to argue," he announced. "Magistrate Summers, I will meet you in the transmodation room. Take the prisoner there at once."

As Summers left with Jean, the villain turned his attention to the remaining X-Men. "One by one, you will all meet your fate," he said with a sneer. "I feel so fortunate to have a front-row seat!"

With a peal of laughter, Hodge left the room. As soon as he was gone, Wolverine used his teeth to pull Hodge's spike from his bleeding thigh.

"You deliberately took those spikes Hodge fired at you," Cyclops said, "figuring rightly that he's the kind who'd never pass up an opportunity to do any of us harm."

Wolverine dropped the spike, catching with his feet. Ignoring Cyclops, he said, "Storm is the thief in our crowd. If she were here, she'd have the lock on these handcuffs undone in no time. Ol' Canucklehead here's just gonna have to do his best."

While his fellow X-Men looked on, Logan lifted his legs above his head. With the spike between his feet, Wolverine went to work on the cuffs.

Click!

The lock snapped open. Wolverine fell out of the cuffs and to the ground—free!

"I'd like to see you beat that, 'Roro," he bragged. "Time to set the rest of you free."

"And find out what Jean had in mind

when she volunteered to become a mutate," Cyclops added.

"I thought I smelled a plot," Archangel said. "Let's just hope we're in time to help her hatch it."

In his laboratory, the Genegineer was just about to clamp Jean Grey onto the transmodation platform. Storm was there, and so were Hodge and Alex Summers. Jean knew that now was the time to act. In a few moments, she would be just another number, another mutate slave.

As soon as the Genegineer came close, Jean shot a swift kick at his face. The man went flying backward, and Jean leaped up from the transmodation platform.

Three magistrate guards came running on the attack, but Havok turned on them. The plasma blast he directed at them sent all three flying backward.

"Stay close to me," Havok warned Jean. "Follow my lead, no matter what."

"Alex!" Jean nearly laughed in relief. "You

remembered who you are!"

"I knew you were faking, both of you!" Hodge shouted as he burst into the room. His tentacles lashed out at Jean and Havok. The Genegineer cowered in a corner of the room, afraid to move.

Havok handed Jean his weapon. "I know now that Hodge implanted false memories in me. We've got to get the others. Try to hold him off with this while I blast us out of here."

Hodge was yelling instructions at Storm. "Mutate 20, there's your target!"

While Havok held Hodge off with his energy blasts, the zombie-like Storm approached Jean Grey. Jean froze. She couldn't shoot her former teammate. But what would Storm do to her? At that very moment, the door behind Storm burst open, solving the problem.

"Who called for room service?" Wolverine demanded, a nasty grin spreading across his face. "I got a fist sandwich I'm dying to deliver!"

"Wolverine!" Jean cried. "Cyclops!"

"Mutate 20," Hodge ordered. "Target reassigned. Take out Scott Summers, now!"

Storm turned from Jean Grey to Cyclops. The hurricane gust she called up left no doubt about her powers: they were still there, only now completely controlled by Hodge. Cyclops was knocked to the ground, battered by gale-force winds. Storm approached her teammate. While Cyclops was still down, she placed her hands on his eyes.

Powerful bolts of electricity sparked around both X-Men. The scream that emerged from deep within Scott Summers was ear-shattering.

"My eyes," Cyclops shouted, "they're burning!"

"He's in agony!" Jean cried. "I've got to help him!"

Storm released Scott Summers and turned to face Jean. "Your assistance is appreciated, Jean, but unnecessary," she said. "I am once more myself. In mind, spirit, and body!"

CHAPTER SIX

In the corner of the room, the Genegineer cowered. Hodge realized instantly what had happened. "I see my trusted friend, the Genegineer, made Storm into a mutant time bomb. Now that she has been catalyzed, and her will is her own, I must take you all more seriously!"

Hodge faced Cyclops and the other X-Men. "What a shame your attempt at escaping will fail," Hodge said. His tentacles snapped out and his eyes bulged. "Step right up, heroes. Who will be the first to fall?"

"Actually, Hodge," Cyclops said, "that privilege has been reserved—for you!"

Cyclops collected all his energy. And

then—*vrammp!* His optic blast filled the room with light. Storm's touch had begun to restore Scott's abilities.

"Nasty, nasty," Hodge scolded. "Nice shot, Cyclops. Best I've ever taken."

Cyclops' knockout blast hadn't even fazed the man. He actually seemed to enjoy it! Hodge's smile was wider and nastier.

"Unfortunately for you," Hodge said, "your powers are nowhere near good enough. I will rip through you to get at Storm. And after that, I will destroy the Genegineer!"

"Empty promises," Cyclops declared. He got ready to deliver another optic blast. "I'm prepared to do whatever is necessary to defend my teammates."

"I'd reconsider if I were you," Hodge said. "Your might alone could never defeat me. I will destroy Storm before she can restore any more of you."

"Will you, Hodge?" Cyclops demanded. "That remains to be seen! The rest of you, get back!"

"Cyclops, no!" Storm warned. "Hodge is

right! You can't defeat him by yourself. I alone have the power to aid you. Only my touch can restore your full abilities."

"Restore Jean's power first," Cyclops told her, "then the others. Just don't take too long about it. The more of us with powers, the better chance we'll have against him."

While Cyclops held Hodge off with a steady stream of optic blasts, Storm went to help the others.

"Jean," she said, "take my hand."

As soon as the two women touched, energy began to crackle around them both. White light surrounded them. Jean felt her teammate's power course through her body. Suddenly, her mind was once again receiving telepathic messages—for the first time since Wipeout had removed her powers!

Time was running out. Hodge was advancing on Cyclops despite the optic blasts. "There's no time to help Archangel, Wolverine, or Cable!" Storm told Jean. "Quickly! Use your restored telekinesis while I attack Hodge with wind and lightning. We must drive him

back or Scott will perish!"

In the Genegineer's laboratory, the battle raged on. Cable, Archangel, and Wolverine watched as Jean and Storm fought off Hodge. But Hodge managed to force himself forward, despite their best efforts. Cyclops' optic blasts bounced off Hodge's armored shell. Storm's wind and lightning had no effect either. Even Jean Grey's powers could not hold the villain back.

"The three of you together are very powerful," Hodge admitted as he crawled forward. "But not powerful enough. Hee hee!"

Hodge showered Storm with a hail of spikes. Jean shouted a warning to her teammate and Storm ducked just in time.

"Watch out!" Jean cried. "Those spikes are only one part of his arsenal."

While avoiding Hodge's weaponry, the three X-Men tried to advance on their archenemy. But Hodge had put up a force field that kept them at bay.

Cyclops was right, Storm realized. She had to activate the others' powers. But she dared not turn away from Hodge, lest he destroy Jean and Cyclops.

Suddenly, there was a tremendous roar. The floor beneath their feet shook, and the walls around them vibrated.

"An explosion!" Storm cried. "It's shaken the very core of the Citadel! But where did it come from?"

There was another explosion, and the ceiling above them collapsed onto Hodge. "My laboratory!" the villain screamed. "No!" And then his entire body disappeared beneath the rubble.

"The ceiling!" Jean said. "Is Hodge—?"

"—dead?" Cyclops finished for her. "Buried? Not a chance. He phased through the floor, seconds before the rubble would have buried him."

"What *was* that, Scott?" Archangel asked. "You almost seemed to have been expecting it."

"One of Forge's auto-bombs," Cable guessed. "I think I understand now why he got himself knocked out. He must have known that Hodge could have found out about the bombs during one of his mind probes."

"We should do Forge a favor," said Wolverine, "and wake him up. Meanwhile, 'Roro, d'ya think you could restore my powers? Hodge had that Wipeout creep take away my healing factor. If I can get it back in action, I could really do some damage. I'm dying to sink my claws into that overgrown paper clip."

"My pleasure," said Storm. She took Wolverine's hands in hers. "Archangel, Cable, care to join us?"

Just as Storm was about to restore the X-Men's powers, a figure stepped out of the darkness. It was Mutate 490—Rahne Sinclair. Havok had given her orders to stay hidden in the laboratory. She had observed the whole encounter with Hodge from her hiding place.

"Rahne!" Jean Grey cried. "Come here! Storm will give you back your powers!"

Silently, Rahne Sinclair linked hands with the group.

In a flash of lightning and a crack of thunder, Cable, Wolverine, and Archangel's powers were returned to them. But as soon as her lycanthropic powers came back to her, Rahne Sinclair underwent an unexpected and terrifying transformation. Slowly, she went from being Mutate 490 to Wolfsbane. But in her wolfgirl state, she was larger, more ferocious. Her claws were longer, her fangs sharper.

"'Tis a miracle," Wolfsbane declared. "In this form, I can think again, and react. But something's changed. I have more strength, more power."

Testing the return of her mutant abilities, Wolfsbane tried turning back into her human shape. But she soon discovered that she could not make the transformation.

The X-Men stood by, horrified to see their teammate's fate. "What's happened?" Storm asked. "What have we done?"

"My genemode transformation process must have augmented Rahne's innate abilities," the Genegineer explained. "And now she is permanently fixed in her wolfgirl mode. I told Hodge she would live to destroy him!"

"Ye are right, Genegineer," Wolfsbane said.

"Hodge allowed me to remember who I was, and tae know what was done to me. And now Cameron Hodge *will* die—by my teeth and claws if need be!"

"Looks like we all want a piece of Hodge," Cable said. He shot his gun into the air. "Let's rescue Forge and go after the guy who's givin' out the grief!"

Ten minutes later, the X-Men had roused Forge from unconsciousness and freed him from his cell. At that point, Storm and Cyclops discussed the X-Men's best plan of attack. Havok, Cable, Jean, Forge, Archangel, Wolverine, and Wolfsbane listened closely.

"Hodge's computer center is the heart of his cybernetic body," Storm said. "I remember that from my time as a mutate, enslaved to Hodge. If we take out his computer link, we take *him* out. Forge, Cable, and I can head up there and shut it down. Meanwhile, I'm sure that the rest of you want your shot at Hodge."

"You bet I do," Alex Summers said. "I plan to use my plasma effect with such fury that it melts him into slag!"

"Easy, boy," Wolverine said, baring his claws. "I want my chance, too!"

Cyclops and the others split up. One team paired off and began a full-scale search for Hodge throughout the Citadel. Storm's crew made their way to Hodge's communications center. There, Storm surveyed the damage wrought by Forge's auto-bomb. The massive computer system was buried under a pile of rubble. And yet the red and yellow lights on the main console still shone dimly.

"His main computer is still feeding Hodge information," Forge stated. "Though some of his energy sources have been destroyed, Hodge is barely weakened."

"I can fix that!" Cable said. He shot off several long blasts of ammunition. A row of monitors exploded. But still the main console hummed along. Cable moved closer, and was about to shoot again when a voice called out.

"Stop! Wait!" The Genegineer stood up from behind the computer.

"What are you doing in here?" Storm demanded.

"I want to help!" the Genegineer protested. "Until now, I've done too little to stop Hodge. The time has come for me to help destroy that madman!"

"Great!" growled Cable. "You can start by getting out of my way."

"I must warn you," the Genegineer said. "If anything will lure Hodge to this spot, this destruction of his power source should do the trick."

"Then we need to act quickly," said Storm. She fired off several blasts of lightning at the console. Cable added his own rounds to the destruction. The Genegineer went around the room pulling down shelves, ripping out cords, and kicking in monitors.

Forge, meanwhile, had pinpointed Hodge's location using the villain's own sophisticated surveillance system. The man appeared on the video monitor. Forge saw that Hodge was engaged in a deadly battle with Wolverine and Wolfsbane, who had also managed to find him.

Wolfsbane clung to Hodge's head. "Ye have

done enough harm," she said. "An' now ye will die."

"Not I, wolfgirl," Hodge retorted, "but you!"

Hodge zapped Wolfsbane with a blast of electricity. The wolfgirl fell from Hodge's body, crying out as she went.

"Not so fast, bub," Wolverine said, taking a swipe at Hodge with his claws.

Hodge turned his electricity on Logan. He managed to blast Wolverine out of claw's reach. But then, in the moment of victory, Hodge froze.

"He's shutting down," Forge cried. "We're getting to him!"

"You don't know him like I do. He'll be onto us any second now," the Genegineer warned.

"My computer functions are failing," Hodge mumbled to himself, his eyes glazing over. "They are in my lab. They think they can destroy me. Not so fast, genejokes!"

Hodge disappeared from Forge's screen. "I've lost him!" Forge said.

"No you haven't!" came the villain's cry. He rematerialized before their eyes. Limping on only three working legs, Hodge charged them as best he could.

"You, Storm!" he cried. "It is you who are to blame—you who have restored the X-Men's powers. You are the author of my troubles! And before I leave this room, I will see you dead!"

Hodge's fearsome blast sent Storm flying. His face contorted in pain and anger. He hauled his limping body closer, and spotted his Genegineer.

"You!" Hodge spat. "Traitor!"

"Yes," the Genegineer agreed proudly. "Storm has restored their powers because *I* restored hers. She is my weapon against you. But she is not the only weapon I possess. With their help, *I* will destroy you."

"Never!" Hodge said. "Even with these mutants as your army, it is *I* who will destroy *you!*"

Hodge lashed out with a dozen tentacles. He pulled the Genegineer into his deadly grasp with one swift, vicious sweep.

The Genegineer kept firing his gun, shouting, "If I am destroyed, at least I will take you with me!"

The Genegineer unloaded a spray of fire from his weapon. Hodge used his tentacles to lift the man into the air. "Away from me, human," the villain cried. "You have hurt me more than the others. But I have an innate power to heal myself, an ability which you lack! Goodbye, Genegineer! Parting is such sweet sorrow."

Suddenly, Hodge threw the man away from him. The Genegineer fell to the ground, his neck broken.

"You have harmed me, mutants," an injured Hodge said, turning back to the X-Men. "But not nearly so much as I, in time, will hurt you."

With that, Cameron Hodge's body began to phase through the floor. A moment later, only his head was visible. A second after that, the man slipped away completely. Cameron Hodge had phased out—yet again.

CHAPTER SEVEN

"He's gone," Storm announced. "Hodge has escaped us. But where—?"

"He can't have gone far," Cable said. "Wherever he's hiding, we'll find him."

By now, Wolfsbane and Wolverine had arrived at Hodge's communications lab. "Where'd he go?" Wolverine asked. "Wolfsbane and I tracked him here, but then we lost him."

"Hodge was here," Cable confirmed. "He killed the Genegineer. Then he phased out."

"Where are the others?" Storm asked Forge. "Can you find them on Hodge's surveillance system?"

"I've located them," Forge confirmed.

"Cyclops and Havok are one floor below. Jean and Archangel are outside, circling the building in search of Hodge."

"Send out a warning to them that Hodge is still alive," Storm ordered. "I want you to stay here, Forge, and try to shut down Hodge's computer. Wolfsbane, Wolverine, Cable, and I will split up and search for Hodge."

The teammates split up. Storm and Cable checked the lower floors, while Wolfsbane and Wolverine took the ones above.

Wolfsbane and Wolverine slowly made their way through the Citadel's gloomy corridors. By now, every last magistrate had disappeared. Hodge's army seemed to know, finally, that they had a chance to escape their insane leader. In the distance, they heard the noise of Hodge's mechanized body. The sound came closer. Wolfsbane and Wolverine turned a corner, and suddenly Hodge himself appeared from the shadows.

"Well, well," the villain exclaimed. "What have we here?"

"It's Hodge!" Wolverine cried into the

transmitter he wore. "Storm, we've found him! Level three, east wing."

"Call for help all you want, mutant," Hodge said. "There is nothing Storm or anyone can do to save you!"

Wolfsbane bared her claws and fangs. She growled, a fearsome sound that filled the hall.

"Get back," Wolverine warned. "You can't attack him single-handedly."

"I'll kill him with my bare teeth and claws!" Wolfsbane could barely contain her anger. She stood on her hind legs, prepared to attack. "That man is my enemy, and he shall pay for what he has done to me!"

Several floors above, Storm and Cable could hear Wolfsbane's strangled cry. "Wolverine, try to control her," Cable shouted into his transmitter. "You're too far away for us to reach quickly. Unless—" Cable went over to a metal grate attached to a wall. He kicked it in, revealing the airshaft. "With your wind power, we can fly there in an instant," he told Storm.

Down below, Wolfsbane was already on Hodge. She grabbed his main link—the one that ran from his body to his head—held it between her paws, and bit down.

"Yeoooww!" Hodge cried. "The shapeshifter plans to sever my neck wires, eh?" Hodge snapped back the wire, flinging Wolfsbane across the hall. "But teeth are no match for technology!" Hodge added.

"Oh yeah?" Wolverine said, approaching Hodge. "How's your technology stand up to my adamantium?"

Wolverine bared his claws. Wolfsbane's massive bite had started to fray Hodge's central link. Wolverine took a long, vicious swipe at the same spot.

"Eeearrgh!" Hodge wailed. "Since you now present a more challenging target—"

At that moment, Cable's head appeared from the airshaft above Hodge. Wolverine was about to warn his teammate when Hodge himself looked up.

"I thought I heard vermin scuttling through the vents," Hodge called out. "I know you're there!"

Hodge stabbed his tail through the air. Its

tip impaled Cable in the stomach. Storm reacted immediately. She flew from the air shaft and cried out, "Monster, release him! You swore vengeance against *me*, Hodge. *I* restored the X-Men's powers."

"How gratifying, weather-witch, to face you at last." Hodge snapped his tail back, flinging Cable to the ground.

Before he lost consciousness, Cable barely managed to yell a warning to Cyclops through his transmitter.

"Cyclops, hear me...Storm's fighting Hodge. She needs help..."

Down below, Scott Summers heard Cable's warning. Jean Grey, Havok, and Archangel were at Cyclops' side, and all four responded to the call.

"We'll be there!" Cyclops cried into his transmitter.

"They're not far, Cyke," Archangel said. "I can hear Storm's thunder. I'm on my way."

Archangel flew off to help his teammates. By now, Hodge had trapped Storm back inside the airshaft and was shooting deadly laser beams at her.

"Admit it, Storm," Hodge crowed, "I have you boxed into a corner. The space is too small for full utilization of your powers!"

Storm knew he was right. She could barely maneuver enough to create wind effects. Meanwhile, she was taking hit after hit from Hodge. In a burst of energy, she finally managed to hit Hodge with her lightning—taking out his laser.

"My laser gun may be gone," Hodge said, "but there is no escape for you!"

Hodge reached out a tentacle, and wrapped Storm in an unbreakable grip. The villain plucked her from the airshaft. Storm struggled against the tentacle, but it was no use. She had just about given up when a voice behind Hodge cried out: "Drop her, Hodge!"

"Well, well, Archangel." Hodge faced his mortal enemy. "You want me to drop her, Warren, old friend—then make me!"

Archangel assessed the situation. From what he could tell, the mechanisms that controlled Hodge were located at the back of the monster's cybernetic body.

The X-Man flew at Hodge, aiming for his rear. As Archangel neared, he sliced at Hodge's back with his glittering wings. In a shower of metal, the back half of Hodge's body exploded.

"You think me immobilized?" he cackled. "Snared? Unable to escape? Mutant fool! You may have destroyed my ability to phase, but I still have my other weapons!"

With that, Hodge opened his mouth. From a jet at the back of his throat, he sent forth a stream of ugly green liquid.

"A polymer I designed, Warren," Hodge explained modestly. "A molecular adhesive."

By now, Hodge had dropped Storm. Archangel went to help his teammate, but Hodge's green muck stopped him short. His wings were glued shut!

"Your death, unlike that of the others, will require my undivided attention," Hodge gloated. "I want to savor it!"

Hodge bound Archangel with his tentacles. Then a buzz saw emerged from the front of the villain's body. Hodge aimed the saw at

Archangel, its blade in a deadly whir.

"And now," Hodge announced, "I will use my saw blade to slice off *your* head. As you once used your wings to slice off *mine!*"

The blade was close enough for Archangel to feel its breeze. In another moment, he would be history. Suddenly, a blast of energy shattered the saw.

"Havok!" Archangel cried.

"Drop him, Hodge!" Alex Summers said.

"Come to save your little friend?" Hodge asked. "Sorry to disappoint you, mutant, but I'm not giving up this prize, even for you. I will gladly destroy the both of you together!"

Hodge aimed the thick blade of his front tusk at Havok. He raised the weapon and brought it down—

"No!"

—onto an empty spot on the ground.

A telekinetic bubble had moved Havok to safety. "Good work, Jean," Cyclops called. "Your telekinetic shield saved him."

Jean and Cyclops marshaled their team. Wolverine and Wolfsbane joined them. Havok pried Archangel from Hodge's tentacles. All together, the X-Men went at Hodge. Cyclops turned his optic blast on the man. Havok sent more plasma his way. Jean protected her teammates with telekinetic shields, allowing Wolverine and Wolfsbane to get close to Hodge.

"Your claws are sharp, Wolverine," Hodge taunted, "but mine is sharper!" Hodge impaled Wolverine on the end of his tail. He lifted him into the air and said, "And far more deadly!"

"Aaargh!" Wolverine cried out. "Someone get me down from here!"

"Logan! I've got you," Jean Grey said.

"Think again, poor sweet Miss Grey." Hodge zapped Jean, forcing her to drop her telekinetic shield from Logan. She fell to the floor, unconscious.

"Jeanie!" Wolverine cried. Screaming in pain, Wolverine used his berserker fury to claw through Hodge's tail spike. Cyclops provided an optic blast as backup, pounding Hodge at the base of his tail. Havok was by his side, sending out one plasma blast after another.

"That's it, Cyke," Wolverine told them. "Keep pourin' it on. Havok! Get this bum where it hurts!"

"It's working, Scott," Havok told his brother. "Hodge is headed for the roof."

Sure enough, Hodge was limping toward a set of stairs that led to the roof. The pain on his face was evident. His crablike body had been ripped in half by Archangel's wings, and blasted by Scott and Alex Summers. Wolverine's claws had sliced through his tail spike. Wolfsbane's teeth had ripped through his neck. But he was still alive, and he was making his escape!

Wolverine hobbled over to where Jean Grey was lying. Cyclops was already there, making sure she was okay. "How is she?" Wolverine managed to say.

"Alive," Cyclops said. "What about you?"

"Been better," Wolverine admitted wearily. "Healin' factor ain't what it was. But we've got Hodge on the run. An' I'm game ta..." Wolverine collapsed to his knees. "...finish him..."

"Wolverine!" Wolfsbane cried. "Ye're in

nae shape tae fight!"

"Neither is Jean," said Cyclops. "Take the communicator. Havok and I are best suited to battle Hodge."

"It's only fitting," Cable agreed. His bionic arm had suffered damage in the fight with Hodge. Archangel's wings were still glued together. Storm was suffering from shock. Of all the X-Men, Havok and Cyclops had the best powers to beat Hodge. They could blast him from a distance and still survive his attacks.

Cyclops and Havok followed Hodge to his rooftop hideout. He looked badly beaten.

"It's over, Hodge," Cyclops said. "Admit it! The X-Men are free—our powers are restored. Your agenda is finished!"

Even in his broken-down state, Hodge was unwilling to give up the fight. "Don't count on it, Scottie!" he cackled. "Even now my circuits are repairing the damage you have done! Soon I will be good as new—and then I shall wreak my revenge upon you genejokes."

"No way, Hodge," Havok said. "You'll

never kill again. We're here to see to that."

Cyclops and Havok let loose with the most destructive blasts they could. The entire roof exploded in light and sound. But still the man survived. His body was a smoking wreck. The wires connecting his head to his body were zapped and fried. His eyes bulged. The circuits that ran his cybernetic system were pushed to their very limit.

"You think I can be killed, mutant scum," Hodge gasped. "But you're wrong. You've taken your best shot and, as you can see, you've failed. I'm still alive. Functioning. And not to be defeated by the likes of you."

"We've still got some power left," Cyclops said. "Let 'im have it, Alex!"

Cyclops and Havok blasted away. Behind the light and above the roar of destruction, Hodge called out.

"Hit me with the full force of your powers!" the villain shouted. "Tear my body into scrap metal! I will live to destroy you!"

"No matter what we do to him," Havok said, incredulous, "he just keeps on talking!"

Even though his arms ached from the effort, Alex Summers sent forth yet another plasma blast.

When the smoke cleared again, the villain was nothing more than a pile of rubble. Cyclops and Havok had turned his mangled body into slag. Hodge's tentacles lay about him, useless. The wiring that had been his body's lifeline fizzled and died. The only part of Hodge that still lived was his head, lying on the ground. And that head was *still* talking!

"There's nothing you can do to silence me," Hodge said. "I am your worst nightmare, for I have made a deal with a demon and cannot die! Even your own death will not protect you. In my hatred I will pursue you, even beyond the grave."

Cyclops couldn't believe it! Hodge's head lay in a pile of slag. His lips contorted wildly as he spoke. This was the same head that had survived its battle with Archangel. To kill Hodge, they had to destroy this last remaining part of him.

"Don't count on it, Hodge," Cyclops said.

"You may be our own private nightmare, but it's time to wake up!"

Scott Summers took a running leap at the man. He raised his leg behind him, and put all his fury into a kick that sent Hodge's head flying over the edge of the building.

"Scott!" Havok cried. "We did it! You knocked him over the edge. He must have fallen 160 stories. Nothing can survive that."

Havok leaned over the edge of the building to make sure Hodge was indeed dead. Suddenly, Hodge's tongue wrapped itself around his neck.

"Aak!" Havok said, losing his balance. "Hodge! Pulling me over..."

Cyclops raced to his brother's aid. Cameron Hodge had one last trick. He was trying to take Havok down with him. Hodge finally released his tongue-hold on Havok, leaving him hanging precariously from the edge.

"Don't worry, Alex," Scott said. "I've got you."

Wedging his foot against the rooftop ledge

for balance, Scott grabbed his brother's hand.

"Do you, Cyclops?" Hodge asked from below. "Do you really? Don't you see that the ledge holding you up won't support you?"

Cyclops felt his grip on Havok begin to slip. Hodge was right. The ledge supporting him was crumbling apart.

"He's right, Scott," Alex said, wincing. "Let go of me. Save yourself."

"No way, Alex!" Cyclops said. "I won't lose my brother."

"Fraternal love! How sickeningly human," Hodge remarked nastily. "I shall survive, of course, while you little heroes will be splats upon the concrete!"

The ledge crumbled more. "I can't hold on!" Cyclops said. "We're going down!"

Cyclops felt himself being pulled over the edge. Havok's hand was still in his, and the ground was far below. He couldn't believe Hodge had won. Was *this* how they would die?

Down below, the X-Men watched the deadly battle. At a glance, Jean Grey understood what was happening. She also knew exactly what to do.

"Think again, Cameron," she muttered. And then she sent out a telekinetic shield that caught Havok and Cyclops. Suddenly, the two X-Men stopped falling. Jean used her powers to lower them to the ground.

Hodge, however, was another story. For the longest time, his head fell from the sky. Finally, it landed, bounced several times, and stopped at the feet of Wolfsbane.

"Hee hee hee!" Hodge's head cackled. "What a ride!"

"Ye!" Wolfsbane snarled. "Ye're still alive!"

"All the better to torment you, my dear!" Hodge's head announced.

"No!" Wolfsbane picked up the head and ripped the wiring from it. "I would nae be so certain of that, monster!" she said. And then she hurled Hodge's head back into the sky.

"Silly little mutate," Hodge's head sang as it flew through the air. "That won't work. Nothing you can do will silence me!"

Suddenly, Forge appeared from the gates of the Citadel. "Stand back, everyone!" he

warned. "I've got this place rigged to blow."

"And Hodge is gonna go with it," Wolverine added. He picked up Hodge's fallen head and hurled it through the Citadel's open gates. "Let's do it, Forge! If we can't kill 'im, we'll bury him!"

Seconds later, Hodge's entire base exploded from a dozen bombs. The Citadel fell in upon itself. One hundred and sixty stories of rubble came crashing down. And Hodge's head was in there, somewhere.

The X-Men surveyed the damage. "There's no way anyone, anything—not even Hodge—could survive that," Storm said quietly.

"Now that this bleedin' place is finally destroyed, we can all go home," Wolverine said.

"Except me," Havok said, surprising them all.

"Alex—" Scott said. "Why?"

"I want to make certain that the mutates who live here are no longer exploited," Havok said. "Not by Hodge, or anyone."

"I'm staying as well," Wolfsbane said. "I'm

a mutate meself. My place is here, with these people. I need tae help them and tae insure that some good comes of the horror that was done tae me, and tae the others."

Cyclops embraced his brother while Storm and the others said their goodbyes.

"This country has been freed from slavery," Storm declared. She stood surveying Hodge's ruined Citadel. "But it has been at a terrible cost. I only hope that Wolfsbane and Havok are right, and that a greater good will continue to be served by this sacrifice."

Beneath the blue Genoshan sky, the rubble of Hodge's Citadel loomed as a reminder of what they had fought. Somewhere inside lay what remained of Cameron Hodge. As they prepared to leave Genosha, the X-Men held the hope that when—and if—they returned, something new and pure would have grown out of the chaos left behind. That Hodge's demented, vengeful ideas would be buried, along with him, in the rubble of his Citadel. And that Hodge was defeated—forever.

BOOKS IN THIS SERIES